The Secret
Life of
Dagmar
Schultz

The Secret Life of Dagmar Schultz

LYNN HALL

CHARLES SCRIBNER'S SONS
NEW YORK

This novel is a work of fiction. Names, characters, places, and incidents are either the product of the author's imagination or are used fictitiously. Any resemblance to actual persons, living or dead, is entirely coincidental.

Charles Scribner's Sons Books for Young Readers
Macmillan Publishing Company
866 Third Avenue, New York, NY 10022
Collier Macmillan Canada, Inc.

Printed in the United States of America
First Edition   10 9 8 7 6 5 4 3 2

Library of Congress Cataloging-in-Publication Data
Hall, Lynn.
    The secret life of Dagmar Schultz.
    Summary: Trapped in a dead Iowa community with no decent boys her age, twelve-year-old Dagmar invents a fantasy boyfriend, who gets her in terrible trouble when he argues with her and makes her talk back to him in front of family and friends.
    [1. Imagination—Fiction. 2. Iowa—Fiction.
3. Humorous stories] I. Title.
PZ7.H1458Sd 1988 [Fic]   87-28499
ISBN 0-684-18915-1

The Secret
Life of
Dagmar
Schultz

One

Hah. I bet you thought you were going to read something really juicy in here, didn't you? The secret life of Dagmar Schultz. Red hot love stuff all over the place, or at the very least some international spy stuff.

Boy, did you pick up the wrong book!

Listen, hospital babies in incubators have more of a secret life than I do. Pond scum amoeba, on microscopes in the high school science lab, have more privacy than I do.

There are two big problems here. One, nothing ever happens to me that's worth keeping secret, and two, if it did, I couldn't. Not in this town, and not in my family.

I could go to Arabia as an exchange student, say

1

for instance. I could get off the plane in Arabia, get kidnapped by a sheik, spend six months in his harem, come home, get off the bus in front of the cafe, and Mrs. Meyer would say to Ethel Johnston, loud enough for the whole county to hear, "There goes that oldest Schultz girl, home from six months in a harem in Arabia with a sheik who had a mole on his butt."

Then I'd walk down the street toward home, and Denny at the gas station would yell out, "Hey there, Dagmar, how'd you like it down there in Arabia in the harem? What'd the crops look like around that country? They get more rain than we been getting here?"

And then I'd walk into my house, and Mom and Daddy and the little kids, Uncle Dean and Aunt Dorothy and my cousin Neese would all be sitting around the kitchen. Uncle Dean would give me a poke in the gut and do his donkey-laugh and say, "Our little girl is sure growing up. Six months in a harem in Arabia, that'll do it every time. Look at the roses in them cheeks." And he'd pinch my cheeks. And Aunt Dorothy would say, "Why, Vesta, I believe she's gone up to a thirty-two A," and she'd pat my chest just like she had a right to. And my cousin Neese would say, "Did you start shaving your legs yet?"

This is no lie. This is exactly what my life is like. So you can see why having a secret life got to be so important to me. It got to be the only thing I wanted. Well, a secret life and my thirteenth birthday. A secret life, my thirteenth birthday, and a boyfriend.

I knew the thirteenth birthday would get there. Only two more months to wait. I had hopes the boyfriend would materialize shortly after the Big One-Three. But the secret life . . . that was the impossible dream.

There are two big things working against me here, my family and this town. I live in New Berlin, Iowa. Only they pronounce it *Ber*lin, like Merlin. It's about halfway between Strawberry Point and Elkader. I don't know if you ever heard of either of those. It's a little bitty town, sits down in a river valley with big hills all around it. There are two blocks of Main Street, but a lot of the stores closed up years ago. At the moment there is one live gas station, Mrs. Meyer's cafe, which is open when she feels like opening it, a branch bank, post office, a library that's open two afternoons a week. One tavern, four churches, seven antique shops.

The people who live here are mostly retired farmers who moved to town when their younger generations took over their farms and needed the farmhouses for their own families. There are a few younger families, like ours, who live here because houses in a little town like this cost about half what they would in a big city like Cedar Rapids or Dubuque.

3

The point is, nobody in this town has a whole lot to do with their time. They sit around the cafe talking about one another, the weather, and the crops. They stand around the gas station talking about each other, the weather, the crops. They lean on the post office wall and talk about . . . well, you get the picture. I'm sure it's nice for them that they don't live under the pressures of big city life and regular jobs and all that, but it makes it just about impossible to do anything that doesn't get noticed and commented on.

"That oldest Schultz girl's walked around that block three times already this morning. Reckon she's going after Matthew Garms, trying to get his attention. She's wasting her time on that one. He can't see beyond that four-wheeler of his."

See what I mean?

And my family is worse. My folks like to say we're an old-fashioned family. What they mean is big. Six kids. Nobody has six kids anymore. I think they were trying to be the Waltons or something. When I complain about it they make jokes and say, "The first one come out so good we just didn't want to stop." That's supposed to butter me up. It doesn't work.

Although they are right. I think I'm going to be quite a woman eventually. Everything's still under construction, but the signs are looking good. For one thing, my name. Dagmar. I love it. It's for some movie star, and sometimes I say it low and husky, with one hand on my hip and my shoulders turned crossways. DAAAAGmar. And then I swing my hair around till it covers about half my face, so nobody can see the evil thoughts flashing through my brain.

I've got very long hair, sort of ordinary brown that I'm going to put blond streaks in as soon as I can get away with it. Mrs. Meyer at the cafe keeps telling me, "If you're going to run around with hair down to your fanny, at least *comb* it once a month and keep it out of your face. Why don't you put it in braids?"

She's so stupid. The whole point of having beautiful long hair is so you can hide in it when you want to. And so people will think you're beautiful. See, I'm not sure about the rest of my looks. I might very well turn out gorgeous. There's still time. But for now, my hair is my best advantage.

I'd kill for a waistline.

But I started to tell you about my family. My dad is Earl, called Early for short. I've heard a few people around town say they think he should get a job. Heck, he's got four jobs, what more do they want? In winter he drives the snowplow for the town, helps put up the Christmas lights on Main Street, sands the steps of the Catholic church on icy mornings. In summer he mows weeds along the highway, for the town. He mows the park and the cemetery, cuts down dead elm trees in people's yards, and works up the logs into firewood.

5

He helps out at the gas station when Denny, the guy who runs it, needs extra help. And on Thursdays he drives the senior citizens' van, so the old ladies around town can get to the bank and post office and grocery store. I lost count. That's more than four jobs, isn't it? On top of those, he runs traplines and hunts coon and gets an occasional deer out of season, on Uncle Dean's farm, and dresses out the meat for our freezer, but if you tell anybody I said that, I'll deny it and call you a liar.

Anyway, that's my Daddy. He's a small man, way older than Mom. He's kind of leathery and cordy, and he's got false teeth on top that don't match the rest of his face. He can always stop the little kids' crying by making his teeth pop out. They get to laughing so hard at him they forget about braining each other.

Mom is lots bigger than Daddy. She's bigger than just about anybody I know. But she promised me I won't get fat like her when I grow up. She had poor nutrition when she was a baby and it made lots of extra fat cells. Or something. Oh, well, being fat doesn't seem to bother her. Mom is a baby person. She just loves babies. Right now her whole world is wrapped up in Delight, my baby sister. Mom has us kids, worships us while we're little, then sort of loses interest when the next baby comes along. It used to hurt my feelings a lot, till I saw her doing it to Cootie, then

6

GeorgeAnn, then David and Deaney. So it wasn't just me personally she lost interest in.

Cootie is my closest brother. He's eleven, and no, you're right, his real name is not Cootie, it's Chuck. He had a little problem with head lice in second grade and got the nickname. It doesn't seem to bother him. The only thing in life that bothers him is me. Cootie and I are natural enemies.

Then below Cootie is my sister GeorgeAnn. You wouldn't like her. Nobody does. Luckily for her, she's so in love with herself she doesn't notice she's in it all alone. She's nine.

Below her are David and Deaney, seven and six. They do everything together, so they're not too much bother to me. And then there's the baby, Delight, who's just starting to walk now, so we can't have tablecloths hanging down.

That's the main family, but on top of them I have all those other prying eyes and big mouths to contend with. Uncle Dean and Aunt Dorothy, who think everything I do is adorable and OPEN FOR DISCUSSION. And their daughter, my cousin Denise, Neese for short, who is four years older than me but doesn't know everything, contrary to her own opinion.

There are also grandparents, other aunts and uncles and cousins, old family friends who feel like they have the right to comment on, and criticize, everything I do. But if I started naming off the whole herd, you'd give up on this, and go read some stupid romance novel instead.

My whole point here is that twelve years and ten months is a hard age to be, even if you could be it in private, but that there is no such thing as private in my life.

Which is probably why I did the stupid thing I did that got me into this mess.

Two

It was Saturday afternoon and Shelly and I were sitting in the river. She's my best friend. Michelle Harbaugh. She used to go by Mickey, but since she got interested in boys she changed it to Shelly.

She's rather cute, I have to admit, although I'd rather not. She's very thin-boned, and she's got short red hair and brown eyes and kind of an elf look that she uses to her advantage whenever she can. She also has freckles all over and wrist bones that stick out in big bumps. Once she tried to tell me she'd broken her wrists falling out of a high tree, but her mother said she never did. She just has big lumpy wrist bones and doesn't like to admit it.

Her being cute never used to bother me. I

9

didn't notice it much when we were little kids, but by now it was beginning to worry me. I mean, I plan to be gorgeous myself, so cute shouldn't bother me. The trouble is, boys aren't smart enough to see that. They just go for whomever can flirt the best, and so far she was ahead of me on that.

It was the second week of September, but we were having a stinky hot weekend, and most of the town was down around the river. The Volga is just a little bitty river that goes through the middle of town. It's nowhere near as big as the Turkey River, and it's hardly spit-sized compared to the Mississippi a few miles east of here. But we like it. It's got clean water and a sand bottom, and it's just about deep enough to wade in. The town park is along one side of the river, with a shelter house, a few picnic tables, and a put-in place for canoes.

Upstream from us there's an old mill and a dam, just a little one you could walk across with no danger. A bunch of men and boys were up there, above the dam, fishing. Washing worms, more like. Too hot and sunny for the fish to be biting. My brother Cootie was up there somewhere.

In the shallow place between the dam and the bridge were three or four mothers with little kids, wading and splashing around. Shelly and I had been sitting on a picnic table talking, but some people came along and looked like they wanted the table, so we left our shoes on the

10

bank and waded into the knee-deep water. We sat down on a submerged sandbar in our shorts and tank tops and just let everything get soaked. It felt great.

We sat there for a long time, with the water rocking us and petting us as it went by. I watched my leg hairs floating like miniature hands waving bye-bye. Time to start shaving them off, I decided, and waved bye-bye right back at them.

Now this was no small decision, I want you to know. I was in a steaming rush to grow up, I'll admit that, and I wanted to do all the woman-stuff as soon as possible. But leg-shaving is forever. Once you start doing it, man, you have to *do* it the rest of your life till you get so old your legs get bald. Whether you feel like it or not, once a week you have to get in there with the old razor and scrape away, or else you get ugly black stubblies all over, and everyone looks at you and thinks, *she needs to shave her legs*. And when you get dressed up in hose you've got big black hairs sticking straight out through the hose.

So I was just making this big decision, and noticing that Shelly still had furry legs and that if I hurried up and did mine I'd be ahead of her on this one. And then we heard it. We both looked up and followed the sound like bats using radar.

It was a four-wheeler.

It came bouncing over the crest of the riverbank and down the path to the flat stretch of weeds and sand, beside the water. God did exist and he was kind!

It was Matthew Garms on the four-wheeler.

Now, if you were to line up Matthew Garms in a row with a hundred fourteen-year-old boys, and then go along picking out the ones you wanted for a boyfriend, he would probably be about your seventieth to eightieth choice. Luckily for him, he doesn't have that kind of competition around here. There are maybe three boys in New Berlin that would be within any kind of reasonable age range for Shelly and me. Matthew was the pick of the bunch, but only because the other two were worse.

Matthew is kind of big and soft around the middle, and whatever he's wearing is always dirty across the stomach, tee shirts or whatever. He has dark hair that grows down very low on his forehead and a kind of a monkey mouth, you know the kind that puffs out just above his mouth, and then the lips are thin and straight. He is not what I'd want for my first kisser.

On the other hand, you have to learn on somebody, and I could feel Shelly gearing up beside me. We both splashed out of the water and waded over to the bank, where Matthew was roaring back and forth, making the four-wheeler bounce up in the air over a little sand dune.

I could tell from the way he wasn't looking at us that all this roaring and bouncing was aimed at us.

He came skidding up to us and did a spin-stop that plastered both of us with thrown sand. I was trying to think of an opening line as he cut his motor, but Shelly beat me to it.

"When you going to take me for a ride on that thing?" she asked in a sickening cute voice.

He didn't say anything, but he turned six shades of red and motioned her up on the seat behind him. With a show-off amount of roar they took off, Shelly hugging and screeching over the sand dune bump.

"Stone cold dead in the water," I told myself. "Dagmar, you are stone cold dead in the water. You're never going to compete with all that cuteness."

Matthew Garms was not, shall we say, loaded down with brains. I didn't figure he'd have the smarts to look at me and see the first-class knockout I plan to be, a few years down the road. Oh, no. He'd fall for the first huggy squeeler that got on his four-wheeler and went over a sand bump with him. And Shelly'd beat me to the draw on that one.

Okay, I thought. Strategy. If I follow her act I'll just be following her act. What I need is to do something totally different to get his attention and show him where the real class was here.

I'd stick up my nose and tell him I never rode anything less than a full-fledged motorcycle.

No, that would just get him mad.

I'd tell him I wasn't feeling well. Yes. That would be much better. "No thanks, I'm not feeling very well today."

I swung my hair in close around my face, sucked in my waistline, and said in a softly regretful voice, "No thanks, I'm not feeling very well today."

Yes. Perfect.

I held my stance as the four-wheeler roared up to me and Shelly slid off.

I rehearsed my line again in my head.

Shelly said, "That was terrific, Matty. Thank you."

Matty? She was calling him Matty? Stone cold dead in the water.

I waited for him to offer me a ride so I could say my fascinating line and get his attention away from her. But he kept looking at Shelly.

She said to me, "Why don't you go for a little ride, Dag? Matty'd take you."

He didn't say anything. He was still looking at Shelly.

All or nothing, I thought, and said loudly, "I'm not weeling fell."

Silence.

Shelly said, "What?"

I turned and waded away into the river.

Shelly caught up with me an hour or so later, by the ball diamond at the other end of the park. There was a game going on, which gave my face

14

something to point toward while I thought my black thoughts behind my hair.

Women's softball is big sport around Clayton County. My Aunt Gretchen was playing today, on the Happy Auto Body Shop team. She works there part-time as a bookkeeper, but mainly they keep her on the payroll because she's the best pitcher in the county. Aunt Gretchen is Mom's sister. She's not exactly fat, like Mom, but Daddy says she's built like a quarterback. She has very short hair and a mole on her lip with the three longest face hairs I've ever seen, growing out of it. She used to be married, but she kept beating up on her husband so he ran off with the dispatcher from the trucking company he worked for. The dispatcher had four kids under school age, but that must have seemed better to him than Aunt Gretchen beating on him all the time.

The Happy Bodies were playing the Garnavillo Gazelles, and judging from the amount of yelling it was probably a pretty good game. I couldn't have cared less.

I couldn't stand to think how stupid I'd sounded in front of Matthew. And the worst of it was, he wasn't even *worthy* of me. To make myself feel better, I started thinking about the kind of guy that would be worthy of me, and how not-stupid I would be in front of him, if I ever found him.

He would be dark-haired like Matthew, but slim through the waist. Big shoulders, though. And brown—no, blue eyes. Yes. Definitely blue eyes with long thick black eyelashes. I warmed up, just picturing him. His name would be . . . Doug. No, Scott. No, Doug. He would have warm kind eyes, and he'd think everything about me was perfect.

I was just getting into the daydream when Shelly climbed up on the bleachers and plopped down beside me.

"Why didn't you want to ride Matthew's four-wheeler?"

I didn't want to talk to her. Behind my hair I was getting this clear picture of Doug, and I wanted to relish him in private for a while.

"Oh," I said in a soft, airy voice, "I didn't think Doug would want me riding with some other guy."

Shelly stared at me. "Who the hell is Doug?"

"My boyfriend," I said with a dreamy smile.

Daddy always told me the smart fish never get caught because they know when to keep their mouths shut. I haven't learned that lesson yet.

Three

You can't miss the Schultz house. You come into town on County Road C, hang a right at the stop sign (there's only one stop sign), go a block, cross the bridge, go another block past the park and the school, and there we are on the left, the most colorful house in town.

It's a two story L-shape with fancy gingerbready carved stuff up under the points of the roof. One side of the house is bright turquoise halfway up and white above that, where Daddy didn't finish painting it. The front and one other side are tan with brown trim, from another time he didn't finish painting it, and the back is dirty white where it hasn't been painted as long as I can remember.

There's a fancy garage that used to be a barn

back in the old days, and there's an outhouse that used to be an outhouse back then, too. Of course we don't use it for that, we use it for garden tools. One time Daddy got silly and put an old television antenna on its roof. Sometimes people from out of town stare at it when they drive by, and you can just hear them saying, "Those people have an *out*house with a television in it!" We laugh a lot about that.

Shelly came home with me after the ballgame, still bugging me about Doug.

"He's a secret," I told her, and immediately I realized I had one of my big wishes. A secret life. Of course it wasn't real, Doug wasn't real, but he was a secret, and I got all charged up about that.

"Why is he a secret?" she demanded as we walked across our front yard and climbed the porch steps. Mom was on a blanket in the front yard, playing with Delight and waving at cars, so she didn't interrupt us.

"Shhh," I said as we went into the living room. David and Deaney were in there playing Monsterman. We stepped over them and went upstairs to my and GeorgeAnn's room. She was there on her bed, reading. I'd describe her to you except she doesn't look like anything.

We had to walk through her half of the room to get to my half, which you could tell by the chalk line across the floor, over the dresser, and up the wall. A chalk line is okay for giving me a reason to yell at her if one corner of her thrown-off clothes gets over the line into my territory. But it's no good at all for private talking.

If we'd started whispering, GeorgeAnn would have stayed forever with her ears stretched over the top of her book, listening, so Shelly and I started talking and laughing real loud, about dumb stuff, till finally GeorgeAnn gave this huge sigh, slammed her book shut, and stomped out.

"Now," Shelly said as we settled down into my unmade bed—I can't stand to sleep in a made bed—"tell me all about Doug. Where did you meet him, and why do you have to keep him secret?"

My mind had been working all this time, so I had some answers ready. "They think I'm too young to have a boyfriend," I said, and she nodded. No need to ask who "they" were.

"So who is he and where did you meet him?" she demanded, bouncing.

His face popped into my mind again, just like it had at the ballpark. I hooked my hair behind my ear and smiled like a woman in love. "His name is Doug. I can't tell anyone his last name, not even you. He made me promise. See, he's . . . oh, I guess I can't tell you that, either. Let's just say he's living with some people over by Strawberry Point. I met him out at Uncle Dean's. This friend of his goes with my cousin Neese, and Doug was out there with him."

19

That sounded believable.

Shelly bounced again. "What does he look like? How old is he?"

I felt mildly guilty, fooling my best friend like this, but the story was so much fun I couldn't help myself. And it was spooky how clearly I could see Doug as I talked.

"Black hair, sort of soft and wavy, blue eyes, really bright blue, with long curly black eyelashes you'd kill for. He's got this really soft fine skin with a kind of sheen on it, and no blackheads, no zits, no bumps. He's got a great build. He's sixteen, and he's got his own car!"

That last part really impressed her. It impressed me, too.

But maybe it was too much, because Shelly got a suspicious look on her face. "If he's that wonderful, why would he be interested in you? You're not even thirteen yet."

I blanked out for an instant, then saved myself. I held up one finger and said, wisely, "Ah, but he doesn't know that. For some reason he got the idea I was fourteen."

She giggled.

I could hear voices downstairs, Daddy and Cootie and Aunt Gretchen. She usually ended up over here after her ballgames, drinking beer with Daddy and making happy-body jokes, because of her team tee shirt with Happy Auto Body Shop on

20

it. The baby was yelling, which meant Mom had put her down to fix supper.

Shelly leaned closer. "Did he kiss you yet? How many times have you seen him? What did he do?"

I closed my eyes and remembered the magic of Doug's first kiss. "He took me for a ride in his car, and parked up on Chicken Ridge, and kissed me seven times. He has very smooth lips, thick but not too thick, and they sort of curl up at the corners, and he's a wonderful kisser."

She poked me. "French or regular?"

I unhooked my hair from my ear and hid in it, mysteriously.

From below, Mom yelled, "Chow time, come and get it or I'll throw it away." Well, I never promised you elegant dining when I invited you into this story.

Shelly called home for clearance, and Mom tossed another plate on the table.

Aunt Gretchen stomped into the dining room. She always rattles the dishes when she walks. She grabbed me by the hair and pulled my head back till I nearly fell over. Her way of greeting people she likes. I've never seen how she greets people she doesn't like. I don't think I want to.

"Say there, Hair, how'd you like the game? I saw you up in the bleachers."

Quick, I tried to remember whether the Happy Bodies won.

21

"Great game," I said, hoping for the best.

She gave my hair a yank that almost uprooted it and waved her empty beer can toward Daddy. "Damn right it was a great game. I been saying all season we could take those Garnavillo Gazelles, didn't I, Early? Say, this beer can has a hole in it."

She turned the can upside down to demonstrate, and Daddy fetched her another one from the fridge. "Thanks, Earl the Pearl. Got to keep the body happy, you know." She patted herself on the stomach and gave my hair a rest, which was a relief. Sometimes I think the reason my hair is so long is that Aunt Gretchen has been stretching it all my life.

After three more yells and several trips from the kitchen, Mom finally got us all rounded up. Cootie got in between Shelly and me, which he loves to do for some reason I've never understood. He smelled like fishbait. He always smells like something dead.

Supper was spaghetti. I'd no sooner got a great big pile of it on my plate when GeorgeAnn started in.

"Mommy," she said innocently—she's the only one who calls Mom Mommy and I think it sounds stupid, but no one ever asked my opinion— "Mommy, who is Neese's boyfriend?"

My fork froze in mid-load. I looked at GeorgeAnn and she sent me this little dagger of a look, and I knew, sure as beans, the little creep had been listening outside the bedroom door when I was telling Shelly about Doug.

Mom snorted. "Neese isn't going with anyone, Georgie. Where'd you get that idea?"

I felt Shelly shooting me a look of "Did you make that whole story up?"

I shot her back a look of "Neese's boyfriend is a secret, too," and hoped she got the message.

Cootie said, "Who'd want Neese? Old lard butt."

Aunt Gretchen grabbed him by the hair and pulled his head back. "Listen, buddy," Aunt Gretchen said, "there's a difference between fat and substantial, and don't you ever forget it."

GeorgeAnn couldn't stand to have the conversation get away from her. She said, "I just wondered who Neese's boyfriend is, with the friend that took Dagmar up on Chicken Ridge and kissed her seven times." She could say things like that in the most innocent voice. Well, you can see why nobody can stand her.

Dead silence around the table. In a gentle, reasonable tone, I said, "GeorgeAnn, the next time you stick your big ear to that door you're going to come away with a pencil jammed so far through your head it'll *come out the other side*." To Mom I explained, "I was just telling Shelly about a dream I had, that's all."

They bought it.

After supper, while the rest of us were clearing

23

the table and doing dishes, GeorgeAnn performed, which she does any time there's company of any kind, even Aunt Gretchen and Shelly, both of whom eat at our house more often than not.

First she played this week's new song on the piano, which is in the dining room. Then she played last week's new song. "The Happy Farmer." Then she played "Over the Waves." Three times, till she got it right. And sang along with herself. Loud.

The thing about GeorgeAnn is she keeps getting louder and louder with every number she does. She starts out like this sweet little girl that has to be coaxed to play for company, but then she gets into it, forgets that people are talking and banging dishes around in the kitchen. She just gets louder and louder.

Finally Daddy yelled at her, over "Twinkling Stars," "Thank you, GeorgeAnn! You've delighted us long enough."

Then he shut the piano lid down fast and she just got her fingers out in time.

Good old Daddy.

Four

I lay in bed that night, with Doug. Well, you know what I mean. He was floating around by the ceiling, talking to me. As long as I was imagining, I made the chalk line into a wall three feet thick with no doors or windows, so GeorgeAnn couldn't listen through.

Doug was getting clearer and clearer in my vision. Not only clearer, cuter. By now he had a kind of a dimple, like John Davidson on television. I could see him whether my eyes were closed or open. I could see him, and see through him at the same time.

Uncle Dean has these slides of their trips, to the Grand Canyon and Silver Dollar City and Lake of the Ozarks, and he's always showing them to people whether they want to see them or not. He has a slide projector but not a screen, so he shows them onto the refrigerator. Once or twice when he got tired of watching slides, Cootie crawled up to the refrigerator and opened the door, so you got 7-Up bottles and dishes of leftovers all mixed in with burro rides down the Grand Canyon. The faces of Mt. Rushmore with a cucumber sticking out a nose.

That's how Doug looked to me. I could see the ceiling through him, if you follow me, like he was a slide projection when there weren't enough lights turned off.

The best thing about him was that he was so intently interested in me. I started this imaginary conversation with him, and it was like he was actually asking me questions.

"What are we going to do tomorrow?" he asked in my daydream.

"I have to go out to the farm," I told him. "They're reshingling the hoghouse roof."

"Sounds interesting," he said, and he sounded like he really meant it. Can you imagine? "I'll go with you and keep you company," he said. "I'll just be in your head. Nobody will know I'm there."

"Hah," I snorted. "They already think I'm about one brick shy of a load. If they knew I was talking to a fantasy boyfriend . . ."

"Beg pardon?" he said politely. Isn't that sweet? Most guys I know would just say "huh?" Doug said, "Beg pardon?"

"What was that about a load of bricks?" he reminded me gently.

"I just meant, you know, one brick shy of a load. Half a bubble off plumb. Not playing with a full deck. The lights are on, but nobody's home. You know. Crazy."

"Ah," he said, and smiled. "They'd think you were crazy for making me up and talking to me? I don't see why. You needed a boyfriend, you got one. And if you ask me, you're better off with me than with Matthew Garms. He needs to do about a hundred pushups every day."

He grinned at me and flashed me his John Davidson dimple, and I melted. He was so cute I couldn't stand it.

He said, "So tell me about this niece of yours that I'm supposed to know."

"What niece? Oh. No, she's not my niece, she's my cousin. Neese."

"Your cousin is also your niece?"

"Her name is Denise," I yelled. And woke up GeorgeAnn, who sat straight up in bed with her hair out in spikes. Imaginary walls don't work. Don't ever depend on them.

"Whazzamatter," GeorgeAnn muttered, trying to get her eyes focused.

"Nothing. I was just having a dream. Go back to sleep."

She growled and flopped over with her back to me and kicked around in the covers to show how mad she was.

I tried to get Doug back, but he was gone. He probably couldn't stand GeorgeAnn either.

We always have to go to church on Sunday mornings. Mom sings in choir, and of course GeorgeAnn sings in Angel Choir, which is kids under ten. Whoever made up the name of Angel Choir never had any kids under ten. I always liked watching Mom up there, though. In her purple choir robe with the gold satin collar thing hanging over it, she looks like some famous opera singer or queen of the Island People or something.

Usually I turn my mind off during the sermon and think about all kinds of good stuff, getting a job so I can buy clothes and makeup, and stuff like that. But today as soon as the sermon started, Doug showed up between my eyes and the program I'd been doodling on.

"Hey, beautiful," he whispered, "you look so pure and saintly, sitting here in church with the sunlight coming in on you through the stained glass. You remind me of the Virgin Mary, with your long beautiful hair."

I just melted.

He got into the pew between me and Daddy and put his arm around me. I almost whimpered out loud, it felt so good.

"What religion are you?" I asked him in my mind.

"I am all religions and no religion," he told me. "I've been to Catholic and Lutheran and Methodist and Hardshell Baptist and Born Again, and I'm working on Hindu and Buddhist now."

"Oh, you are not," I scoffed. "You aren't anything. I just made you up, so I can make you whatever I want. You're Methodist like me, so shut up."

"Okay," he said cheerfully. "This is your fantasy. Who am I to screw it up for you? But I think you should look into Hinduism. You'd like it."

"This is stupid," I said loudly. Suddenly I was aware of silence around me, then titters. I looked up. Reverend Ingham was staring down at me from the pulpit, with his eyebrows three inches higher than usual.

Everyone was looking at me.

I'd talked out loud. In church. During the sermon. And I'd said, "This is stupid." They probably thought I meant the sermon.

To die, to die.

We had Sunday dinner out at the farm, after a quick stop home to change clothes. It was a sunny day, but not nearly as hot as the day before, so the roof shinglers wouldn't have it too bad. You don't ever want to try shingling a hoghouse roof in hot sun. The shingles melt and stick together, and you can get tar burns on your knees. Remember that.

The farm is two miles out of town on the gravel pit road. It was Daddy's family's home place, where he grew up. Gramma and Grampa Schultz sold out to Uncle Dean when they decided to move to Florida. Uncle Dean had been farming it with them all his life anyhow, and he was the one that wanted it. Daddy preferred town living, which is easier in some ways, harder in others.

But the farm felt like my other home. It had a big yellow stone house with green shutters, and all the farm buildings were painted green to match. It was one of the better farms around New Berlin, everyone said that.

In the front yard was a sign that said, Kountry Kut and Kurl. That was Aunt Dorothy's beauty shop, around at the side door. She didn't have too many customers anymore, since a new Sunshine and Hair shop opened up in Elkader where they do chemistry tests on a snip of your hair to be sure they don't frizz you. Aunt Dorothy frizzed people pretty regularly, but most of her customers were old ladies who didn't like to go the whole seven miles to Elkader, and were so used to being frizzy they probably liked it that way.

30

Neese was their only child and heir to the throne of beauty shop queen when her mother retired. Hair to the throne, you might say.

There. Doug laughed just as I was saying that. He was beginning to pop up all over the place.

We were all trekking back and forth from kitchen to dining room table with platters full of stuff when Cootie said to Neese, "Hey, Neese, I hear you got a new boyfriend."

She just stopped walking and stood there, gravy boat in one hand, celery and radish tray in the other. She always wears jeans like weenie skins, and her hips bulge out so she looks knock-kneed even though she's not. She had her hair in some new kind of Afro frizz, probably her mother's work. It made her face look fatter.

And red. Did her face ever turn red when Cootie said that. At first I thought she was just mad or embarrassed, but it got about three shades redder than that, so I had to wonder if maybe she did have something going on that nobody knew about.

"I do not, Cootie-brain."

She put down the food and the moment passed, but I couldn't help wondering.

In my ear Doug whispered, "She looked guilty to me, too."

"What are you, reading my thoughts now?" I shot back at him silently.

31

"Why not?" he shrugged. "I live in them, I should be able to read them."

Face it: when he's right, he's right.

Aunt Dorothy had a big fancy pile of reddish gold hair, with little curls all around her face. I personally thought she'd have been prettier with less makeup, since it made her look old and fakey, but as I say, no one ever asked my opinion about anything.

She called us all to the table, Uncle Dean said the blessing, and we piled in. After dessert, we all sat back sort of belching, except David and Deaney and GeorgeAnn, who took off for outside as soon as they were excused. The men kept on sitting around the table, putting off the shingling, while the rest of us started on the dishes.

Uncle Dean looked over at my bare legs under my shorts and said, "Dagmar's going to have to start shaving the old gams one of these days."

What I really wanted to do was just go into a closet, shut the door, and emerge ten years later as a finished product, the gorgeous broad I intended to be. I really hated having to mature in front of everybody!

"Grin and bear it," Doug whispered.

Neese pulled up one of my arms by the elbow and stuck her finger in my armpit. I was trying to dry the big china meat platter at the time and just about lost it.

"She's getting beards in her armpits," Neese sang.

I put the platter down before I hit her with the towel.

Mom said to Aunt Dorothy at the sink, "I remember when I was her age. I wanted to shave my legs so bad, and my folks wouldn't let me, so I got a tube of that hair remover stuff. You remember how that stuff used to be years ago? Stank to high heaven. Worse than home permanents used to smell."

I'd heard this story before, but I liked it, so I dried dishes quietly and listened.

"I didn't know how much to put on," Mom said, "so I just slathered the whole tubeful on my legs. I bet that stuff was caked on there half an inch thick. Well, then I read the rest of the directions, where it said to leave it on half an hour. Didn't think I could stand the smell that long.

"No sooner had I got it all on me when Mother called dinner. Well sir, there I was, legs plastered like they was both broke and set in casts, Mother calling dinner, and half an hour to go before I could take the stuff off. And trying to keep it a secret because I wasn't supposed to be shaving my legs."

"You weren't shaving them," I said reasonably.

"A fine point, and my mother didn't hold with fine points. I had to go down for dinner, and I didn't want to wash the stuff off. It'd cost me every penny I had, and it would have been wasted if I didn't leave the stuff on for the full time. So I just got out my biggest loosest jeans and pulled them on over that stinky cream and went on down to the table.

"Well sir, then I remembered it was Friday and every Friday we had Reverend Lonsdale and his wife at our place for dinner. Church didn't have much money for salaries back then, so we all tried to help out with meals on a regular basis, and there was Reverend and Mrs. Reverend sitting there waiting for something to disapprove of. That was the kind of people they were. I never liked that man, minister or not."

"So what did you do?" Neese asked.

Mom shrugged. "Nothing I could do. I sat there and pretended I didn't stink to high heaven. Mother commenced sniffing the air, Mrs. Reverend sort of coughed into her hanky. I caught Reverend aiming his nose down for a quick whiff of his armpit just to make sure it wasn't him. Daddy looked at his boot soles. He'd been in the barn and reckoned he'd stepped into something unbeknownst.

"Mother took the stew dish back out in the kitchen, probably scared there was something in the stew that had gone bad. But gradually everybody started looking at me, and it got quieter and quieter, till finally my brother yelled out, 'Vesta stinks!' So then the jig was up, and I had to confess and roll up my pant leg and show them. Seems funny now, but I tell you, at the time I just wanted to disappear off the face of the earth."

I know the feeling.

I shot a look at Mom, thinking maybe she told that story on purpose to make me feel better about talking out loud to myself during the sermon. But I couldn't tell from her face.

Five

It was a nice afternoon and I would have liked to go outside and lie around on a blanket in the yard, but I was afraid if I tried that I'd end up on the hoghouse roof nailing shingles. If they'd let me snap the chalk lines, with the reel of chalky cord to mark the rows, that would have been fun, but nailing shingles or handing them up to the nailers like Cootie and the younger boys were doing—well, I'm sorry but that's just not my idea of fun.

So I took the sexist way out and stayed in the house with the women. Mom and Aunt Dorothy settled down for snore contests on sofa and daybed, so Neese and I went up to her room. One thing Neesie is good at is eye makeup. She did hers with three colors of eye shadow—brown, green, and silver—to show me how she'd learned to accent her lids. I never quite figured out what the point was, of accenting your lids, but she read it in *Seventeen,* so it must be right.

She did mine in midnight mauve with seafoam green highlights, and black lines underneath my eyes. Just between you and me I couldn't decide whether I looked like a foxy chick or a dead raccoon, but it was fun messing around with her stuff. Then she started playing with my hair, like she always did when I let her. She was trying to learn to make that big thick braid that sticks to the back of your head all the way down.

While she combed and I sat in her dressing table chair sneaking peeks at my raccoon eyes in the mirror, Neese said, "Where did Cootie get the big idea that I had a new boyfriend?"

"Do you? Ouch. You turned red as a beet when he said that. I figured he must have hit the old nail right on the thumb."

"No. I don't. There's a guy I like, is all. But nothing's happened yet, and most likely won't. What I want to know is, where did Cootie get that idea?"

She was getting a little rough with my scalp, and it made me grouchy. I didn't exactly feel like telling her I'd made up a fake boyfriend just to show off to Shelly.

"What's this fake boyfriend?" Doug said suddenly from within the mirror. "I may be a fantasy, but I resent being called a fake. I'm the best boy-friend you ever had, Dagmar Schultz."

Neese gave me another yank with the comb and said, "Come on, tell me. Did you tell Cootie I had a boyfriend?"

I was getting a little ticked off with Neese by this time. Doug said, "Tell her about me. That'll make her jealous. Tell her you met me through Shelly. . . ."

I caught on to his drift. With great black-eyed dignity I said, "Cootie wasn't supposed to know anything about it. See, I've got a new boyfriend. He's a friend of a guy Shelly is going with, but nobody's supposed to know about it because both Shelly's folks and mine think we're too young. So we were talking about our boyfriends and GeorgeAnn was listening outside the door, the lit-tle creep, and she told Cootie she'd heard some-thing about a boyfriend, and he asked me, and I told him you had one. You were the only person I could think of, fast, that would be old enough not to get in trouble with their folks, see?"

"You've got the nerve of a rhino, dragging me into it. And I'm going to tell Cootie you lied."

"Okay," I said quickly, "but don't tell him about Doug, will you? That's my boyfriend." I got such a glow, just saying "Doug, my boyfriend," I felt like I'd been eating lightning bugs.

Neese finished her braid, but it felt funny on my head, too loose and sloppy on one side. I told her so and she snorted, ripped out the rubber band, and started over. I wished I'd kept my big mouth shut.

"So tell me about this Doug," she said. "How old is he, what's he look like, how'd you meet him, and what have you done so far?"

Doug gave me the sexiest wink I have ever seen, from where he was floating around in the mirror. "He's sixteen," I said dreamily. "He's got his own car, blue eyes with long curly black lashes, dark hair with sort of soft thick waves. Smooth skin, and the smoothest strongest lips you've ever seen."

"Don't forget the John Davidson dimple," Doug prompted, and flashed it for me. As if I could forget.

"A dimple like John Davidson's, and the sexiest smile. And a kind of a soft, thrilling voice."

Doug said, "Don't forget smart and gentle and thoughtful."

"He's smart and gentle and thoughtful," I added.

"Where did you ever meet a hunk like that around here? Where does he live? What's his last name?"

"Watch it," Doug warned.

Carefully I said, "Well, I met him through this friend of Shelly's, like I said, but I can't tell you any more than that. See, he's from, well, I can't tell you. He's living with a family over by, oh, I guess I shouldn't tell you that either. You could say

39

he's like a foreign exchange student, but not exactly."

Neese snorted. "You make him sound like some kind of international spy or something."

Doug looked thoughtful.

I looked modest and said, "Well, if he was a spy, then you could see why I wouldn't be able to tell you very much about him, last name or anything like that."

Neese bellowed. "You trying to tell me there's a sixteen-year-old spy, in Clayton County, Iowa, and that he's got the hots for my twelve-year-old cousin who's barely got boobs even?"

Doug made a face.

"No, I'm not trying to tell you that," I said cleverly. "I'm not trying to tell you anything. You're trying to pry it out of me."

"There, you're done,'" she said, and patted the braid. "Hey, you know why we have belly buttons? God was going down the assembly line, checking over his first batch of humans. He stuck his finger in each one and said, '*There*, you're done, *there*, you're done, *there*, you're done.'"

She hooted, and I snorted and looked at the braid in the hand mirror over my shoulder. It was a pretty good braid, actually. I could see some advantages in having Neese for a cousin when I really did get a boyfriend and needed good hair styles.

"What do you mean by that?" Doug demanded. "Aren't I good enough for you?"

Silently I snapped back, "You are not *real,* you corncob. I know it, you know it. And I wish you'd quit listening in on my thoughts."

Neese was looking at me oddly. "Your lips are moving," she said. "What are you, talking to yourself now? I mean, you were always a little weird, but still and all . . ."

Doug whispered, "Your niece Cousin is a stupid cow, isn't she?"

I gritted my teeth, held my lips still, and thought to him, "My cousin *Neese.* Can't you get that straight? And don't call her stupid. You're no prize winner yourself in the brains department if you won't even face the fact that you don't exist."

He just grinned his darling dimply grin and said, "I don't like your hair that way. I like it better loose."

I pulled off the rubber band and shook out the braid.

"Hey," Neese bellowed, "I just spent half an hour on that. What are you taking it out for? That was a terrific braid, in case you didn't know it."

"I know. But I thought you were doing it for practice. I didn't want to wear it that way. See, Doug really likes my hair long and loose. He likes to just wrap his arms around me and bury his hands in my hair. When he kisses me," I added, feeling the thrill of those kisses all the way down to my toenails.

Neese looked at me. "You've been out messing

41

around with some sixteen-year-old kid that your folks don't know about? How far have you gone with him?"

I just smiled, and Doug smooched me a kiss. I was turned away from the mirror now, with Neese sitting on the corner of her bed, but Doug had gotten himself over around the window curtain.

"Listen, Daggie," Neese said in a motherly voice, "let me tell you one thing about guys."

"What's that?" I stuck out my skinny hairy legs and turned them to see if they were starting to get any shape yet down the back.

"You can't believe one thing they tell you, especially when they're trying to get you to . . . you know."

I looked up, startled. I hadn't thought about Doug that way, just in a romantic way. For a second I got scared. Then I remembered he wasn't real and rolled my eyes toward heaven at my own stupidity. Here I was, the one who made him up, and even *I* couldn't remember he wasn't real. How could I expect him to?

Neese went on. "It sounds to me like he's been feeding you a line you could catch whales on, kiddie. If he told you he was from some foreign country or he was a spy or some dumb thing like that, then he was putting you on. Trying to impress you so you'd do whatever he wanted. Don't you believe him, you hear me?"

"He's never lied to me," I told her flatly.

42

She sighed. "Kids your age are so gullible. You'd believe anything a good-looking guy told you. Is he really that cute?"

Doug raised his eyebrows and waited.

"He is perfect," I told her honestly. "If I'd been inventing a boyfriend I couldn't have invented a better one."

Neese got a hungry look on her face. "I want to meet him. See if he's got a friend for me, will you?"

Doug ho-hoed over by the curtain.

"I'll ask," I said carefully, "but don't count on it. I really don't think he has any friends around here except me."

"And the one Shelly's going with," Neese reminded me.

"Oh, yeah." I'd forgotten I'd told her that. This was getting complicated. Now I had two stories to keep straight. I'd told Shelly I met Doug through Neese, and I'd told Neese I'd met him through Shelly. And GeorgeAnn and Cootie had their noses and blabbery mouths in on it now, too.

I'm not at all sure you're worth it, I thought, and Doug gave me a snooty look, like he knew darned well he was worth it.

I sighed, and Neese started on me with blusher and cheekbone highlighter.

Six

I don't know how you feel about Monday mornings. They always make me grouchy. For one thing, they come around twice as fast as Friday afternoons.

I was especially grouchy this morning because it was still only half past September and my body wasn't adjusted to school yet. It was still in lazy-summer gear. What I really wanted to be doing, seven-thirty on a Monday morning, was lying in bed thinking about Doug. Not waiting for the school bus in front of the post office.

There is one lucky thing in my life. I don't have to ride the bus with Cootie or GeorgeAnn. The New Berlin school building has the middle school grades, junior high is in Strawberry Point, high school is in Elkader. Lower elementary in Osborne. I know one family that's got kids on four different school buses.

This year Shelly and Matthew Garms and I were the only junior high kids in New Berlin. The bus picked us up in front of the post office because it was halfway between our three houses.

I got there first and flopped down on the bench under the post office window. Another depressing thing was that my homework was not in perfect shape. As usual, I'd left it till Sunday night, and then there was a great eight o'clock movie on television, about a fourteen-year-old girl who runs away from her rich parents and gets caught in a prostitution ring in Los Angeles, so you can see how homework would have lost out in that competition.

"I think I'll go to school with you today," Doug said.

I looked around.

"Behind you," he whispered.

He was in the reflection in the post office window, mixed in with the bank building across the street.

"I don't think so, thanks," I told him. "If I start talking out loud to you in school, like I did yesterday in church, I'll really get my tail fried."

He slid down onto the bench beside me and

started brushing my under-of-chin with a wisp of my hair. "Ah, come on. I'm your dream boyfriend. You're supposed to take me everywhere with you."

Old Charlie appeared around the corner and started shuffling past me. He takes steps about three inches long, so it takes him forever to get anywhere.

He looked at me and grinned like he knew what I was up to, but then he always does that, whether I'm up to anything or not.

"Hi, Charlie."

He nodded and sort of blew his lips in and out, which translates to hi Dagmar, I suppose.

Doug hissed, "Who's that? One of your other boyfriends?"

"Get out of here!"

Charlie paused—with him it's hard to tell pausing from walking—and turned and looked back at me. I gave him a snooty smile. Heck, he talks to himself all the time; where does he get off looking at me like that?

"Yep," Doug said. "I'll have to stay right with you every minute at school. I can see that right now. You've probably got guys looking at you with lust in their eyes, all over the place."

"Oh, come on," I snapped. "If I had real guys, would I have needed to make you up?"

Hah. He didn't have an answer to that one. Score one for my side.

46

Just as the bus came in sight down the street, Shelly and Matthew Garms came running up, together I noticed. And, are you ready for this? He was carrying her books. I mean, how corny. Carrying her books.

"I'd carry yours," Doug said sweetly, "if they were imaginary."

"Imaginary school books? In your dreams, buddy."

We all three or four of us got on the bus, and I was relieved to see that Shelly and Matthew weren't so far gone as to sit together on the bus. That's the most public statement you can make, just about. Short of pregnancy and a forced marriage.

Shelly slid in beside me, in our usual seat. I couldn't see Doug anywhere, but I figured he was hanging out somewhere in my head, reading my most private thoughts.

"So what did you do Sunday?" Shelly asked. But her face was all tied up with wanting to say something, so I figured she just wanted me to get my piddling little Sunday news off my chest so she'd have my whole attention when she told me hers.

Which she did. All the rest of the way to Strawberry. Most of it was too boring to repeat. What it boiled down to was that she and Matthew rode around the timber roads in Nelson's woods all day, and he showed her his deer stands. A deer stand is like a little wooden platform that a guy builds up in a tree by a deer trail, so he can shoot deer and act like a big macho hunter. Probably to a jerk like Matthew, showing you his deer stands is the ultimate intimacy. At least, he must not have tried to kiss Shelly or she would have told me, first thing.

In my right ear, which was by the window, Doug murmured, "Come wiz me, my darling, and I will show you my muskrat trap. My gopher poison."

"Get out of here."

He was in the window, between my face's reflection and the cornfields we were passing.

"The best part," Shelly was saying, "is, guess what?"

I hate her guess-what games.

"I don't know. What?"

"You know the party we were talking about, for my birthday?"

That got my attention. "Yeah? Pajama party like last year?"

She shook her head. Her eyes were so bright they looked Windexed. "Better than that."

I pondered. "Skating party at the roller rink!"

"Better." Her eyes were about to dance off her cheeks.

"What could be better than a skating party?"

"A Real Party. They said I could have a Real Party, with boys and dates and dancing, the whole ball of wax. Isn't that fantastic?"

48

"Yeah, for you," I grouched. "You've got Matthew. What am I supposed to . . . oh."

Open mouth, insert foot.

She hit me on the arm. "You can invite Doug," she crowed. "Won't that be perfect? I'll get to meet him, and we'll have dancing in the moonlight, and all kinds of neat stuff."

Trapped in my own rat trap.

"Caught by your own big mouth," Doug added.

"He can come, can't he?" Shelly asked, seeing my expression.

"Not on your shinbone," Doug hissed in my ear. "A sixteen-year-old hunk with his own car and a John Davidson dimple does not hang out with thirteen-year-old kids at a stupid birthday party."

"Get out of here," I snapped, and swatted at him with my hand.

Shelly looked at me oddly.

"Darned mosquito," I muttered.

"You will bring him, won't you?"

I shrugged and evaded her eyes. "I'll try, Shell, but sometimes he has other things he has to do. I'll just have to see if he's free Saturday night."

She gave me a long hard fish-eye look.

"I think you're lying, Dagmar."

"Lying? Lying? How?"

She thought, then said, "I don't think there's any such person as this Doug, who nobody has even seen. I think you made the whole thing up because you were jealous of me and Matthew."

49

I drew in my breath and my dignity. "I did not. I would never do such a stupid thing. I'd never make up a story like that. And besides, when did I ever lie to you?"

She counted on her fingers. "The time you told me you were adopted. The time you told me you were getting a pony. The time you told me . . ."

"All right, all right. That was when we were little kids."

"You told her you were adopted?" Doug hooted in my ear. "Well, seeing your family, I can understand that."

"What's the matter with my family?" I demanded silently.

"Dag?" Shelly was looking at me again.

I shut off the right side of my brain, where Doug was poking at me, and said, "Believe me, Shelly, Doug is real. A real pain in the *butt* sometimes, is what."

"Then you will bring him Saturday night."

"If he can come."

"And if you don't bring him, I'll know you were lying and made the whole thing up, and I'll never believe another word that ever comes out of your mouth. If you tell me it's raining and we're standing in the pouring rain I won't believe you."

"He'll come if he can," I said with great dignity.

"In a pig's eye," Doug hissed.

For the rest of the bus ride we recited our closets and tried to figure out what to wear to the party. It would have been perfect, under ordinary circumstances with a real live boyfriend, even a lard-bucket with a cow-pie brain, like Matthew.

But this was not ordinary circumstances. This was a Dagmar-disaster in the making.

Seven

During English that morning, I was excused to go to the computer lab and work on my project from last Friday. My Apple had gone rotten Friday and wouldn't show anything but a screen full of !*!*!*!*!*!*!

The assignment was to write a letter to somebody famous and actually send it to him. I decided to write mine to Stephen King, because I love his gruesome movies. And I had an idea for a story that I thought he might want to write.

It was about a thirteen-year-old girl in a small Iowa town who has the power to turn people into frozen statues. First she turns her little sister into a statue just as her hands are getting ready to crash down on the piano to play "The Happy Farmer."

Next she freezes her little brother just as he's getting ready to push open the bathroom door and spy on her while she's on the john. That's what Cootie used to do to me when he was little, and it made me want to choke him to death.

What I was hoping was that Stephen King would write this into a book and split the money fifty-fifty with me for giving him the idea. Then, for the movie, Stephen would come to New Berlin to talk to me about background details, and he'd see that I would be the perfect one to play the lead in the movie. He'd take one look at this long, beautiful hair, and the midnight mauve and seafoam green eyelids with the black raccoon lines, and I'd be in. Probably he'd fall in love with me, too, but he'd be too old to do anything about it, so he'd just worship me from a distance and guide my career.

These thoughts were going through my head as I wrote my computer letter, and I braced myself for Doug's smart-mouth comments. But he didn't show up. I heaved a sigh of relief, took my Stephen King letter, and started back toward my English class, with a quick detour to the girls' restroom. Nobody was in there, since classes were going on. In fact it was such a nice quiet place I got comfortable and started daydreaming about being a teenage movie star. Maybe I could do a music video with my hair standing two feet out from my head, and triangles painted all over my face and arms in sparkly stuff.

"You have to have talent to be a movie star and rock singer," Doug said. "All you've got is a giant imagination."

"Good thing for you I have," I shot back. "Or else you wouldn't exist. Eeeeek! What are you doing in here. You can't be in here, this is the girls' restroom. *Get out* of here."

"You can't make me."

"Doug, get out of here! What's the matter with you, have you got a sick mind or something? You're as bad as my little brother. You get out of here right now or I'm never going to think you up again."

I got up off the john just as another one flushed, down the line somewhere. We met by the mirror, me and Amy Schmelling. She just stared at me, forgot to wash her hands, and out the door she went, still looking back at me.

"Well, thank you very much, Doug. You have really done it to me this time."

He smirked down at me from the mirror.

"Do you know . . ." I dropped my voice to a whisper and looked around the room. All the stall doors were swinging open, so we really were alone now. "Do you know who that was, you corncob? That was Amy the Snitch Schmelling. Tattling is her favorite sport. When we were in third grade Jamie Archer spit on the floor. Everybody saw him do it, but nobody was going to say anything. Except Amy, and she couldn't wait to tell on him.

54

And she smirked the whole time he was scrubbing it up with a paper towel and writing *I will not spit* a hundred times in his notebook. And one time in fourth or fifth grade . . ."

Doug held up his hand. "I get the picture; you don't have to beat me over the head with it. So what's the big deal? You weren't doing anything wrong."

"No. *You* were, hanging around in the girls' restroom. But try and explain an imaginary boyfriend to Mr. Ebersole."

Doug gave a graceful shrug and showed me just a hint of his John Davidson dimple. "Well, sweetheart, if you can't control your talking out loud to me when you shouldn't, you can't blame me for the trouble it gets you into."

I threw up my arms hopelessly.

He went on. "And don't think you're going to get me to take you to your friend's birthday party, either. I'm not going, and that's that."

He was so exasperating! "Doug! Are you as crazy as I am? How could you take me to Shelly's party when *you don't exist?*"

"Oh, yeah. I keep forgetting. Well anyhow, you've got yourself in a corner on that one, Daggie."

"And *don't call me Daggie.* I hate it."

"Well, so what are you going to do about the party? You've bragged me up to the whole world. Now you're going to have to produce me. And even if I was willing to go to such a boring kid-thing, I couldn't since I don't exist, as you so rudely keep reminding me. So what are you going to do?"

I pulled out my comb, combed my hair right into his image in the mirror, and blurred him. Served him right. "What I'm going to do is get back to English before they find out how long I've been in here. And hope to God Amy keeps her mouth shut."

"In your dreams, kiddo. You said she was a snitch. She won't be able to resist this."

I gave him my worst nasty look, but he'd already faded from the mirror. It would sure be nice to have the power to just fade away when you wanted to, wouldn't it?

My marching orders arrived during fifth period, which was study hall. Mr. Ebersole wants to see Dagmar Schultz in his office immediately. Over the loudspeaker, of course, so everybody in study hall heard it and turned and smirked at me.

"I'm going to get you for this," I snarled silently as I walked down the hall. But Doug wasn't anywhere around. Talk about your fair-weather fantasies.

Mr. Ebersole sat me down and smiled at me from behind his desk. He always smiled; it didn't mean anything. I think it was something they taught at principal school. He was a short, fat, bald man, and I mean b.a.l.d. Not even a fringe around

56

the edges. Don't look at him in the bright sunlight, folks, he'll blind you with his shine. And he wore these silly little half-glasses, so he was always dropping his chin down and looking at you over the tops of the glasses.

"Well, Dagmar," he said without disturbing his smile, "I've been hearing some upsetting things about you."

My eyes widened innocently. He motioned to a chair and I sat, hooking my hair behind my ear so he could see that I was facing him openly and honestly, with nothing to hide.

"I understand you were meeting a boy this morning in the girls' restroom." He dipped his head down and stared over his glasses at me. The smile was still there, but it was down among all the chins where I couldn't see it very well.

"No sir, I wasn't. Amy thought she heard me talking to someone, but I was just thinking out loud. Talking to myself."

His scowl deepened. "She heard you call him by name and say, 'Get out of here, this is the girls' restroom,' or words to that effect. How do you explain that?"

Doug whispered, "Honesty is the best policy, Daggie darling."

Well, why not? Give it a shot, anyway. I cleared my throat. "See, Mr. Ebersole, what happened was, a few days ago I started making up this, well, kind of like a pretend boyfriend, see. My best friend Shelly Harbaugh had a boyfriend and she was kind of bragging him up, you know." I smiled my humblest smile, shrugged, and let a lock of hair fall loose beside my cheek, trying for a little-girl look.

"So I just, well, fibbed and told her I had a boyfriend too, and started making up details about him, how cute he was, and that he was sixteen and had his own car, stuff like that."

"Don't forget the dimple," Doug whispered. I scowled and swatted him away from my ear.

"So that's who I was talking to in the restroom. It was this pretend boyfriend. There wasn't any boy in the restroom. Honestly." I shook my head and let loose a little more hair, and met Mr. Ebersole's eyes with the clear, honest gaze of the innocent.

He rocked way back in his chair to stare at me, and his little short legs came up so his feet were swinging way up off the floor.

Doug started singing in a whisper in my ear, "Froggy went a-courting, he did go, um-hmmm . . ."

I held my innocent look, but my face was tightening up. Mr. Ebersole did look exactly like a frog when he sat back in his chair like that, with his feet up in the air and his chins all pouching out, and his little arms having to curve out around his fat little body. I could see him all green and naked, squat-

58

ting on a lily pad catching flies with his tongue and smiling over his half-glasses.

My mouth started twitching and my eyes started sparkling. I fought it. Oh, how I fought it, but one side of my lips came up just a fraction. I hardened my whole mouth in a straight line and tried to take a deep breath.

Doug whispered, "Don't laugh, don't laugh."

I sputtered a teeny sputter.

Mr. Ebersole's smile vanished and his chair rocked forward so his little frog feet touched the floor. "I'm glad to see you're enjoying this, Miss Schultz," he said in an extremely cold voice.

There was absolutely nothing to laugh about now. I was in trouble up to my armpits and I knew it, but I couldn't help it. The laugh twisted around in my windpipe and came up like bubbles in a bottle of pop. I tried to make it into a sneeze or a cough, but I wasn't fooling anybody.

Scowling now, Mr. Ebersole wrote something on a pass slip and handed it to me. "Here. I want you to go down and talk with Dr. Feete. I'll call her office and tell her you're on your way."

The shrink. He was sending me to the shrink.

"And not a moment too soon," Doug said.

Eight

The school psychologist was only at our school a half day a week. We don't have too many crazies in Clayton County, so she covered about ten schools. I'd never seen her up close before, just glimpses in the halls.

She was tallish and thinnish, with tan-colored hair and skin, and no makeup at all. Her hair was sort of middle-length and somewhere between frizzy and curly and straight. No style to it at all that I could see. If I'd been her, I would have used a pile of green eye shadow and a dark brick red lipstick since her lips didn't hardly show up at all.

The thing that almost cracked me up when I sat down in her office was her name plate on the desk. Sandra Feete, Ph.D. You know what that made her nickname, don't you? Think about it for a minute.

I didn't dare think about it. I was in enough trouble from seeing Mr. Ebersole as a frog. I didn't need to start picturing her with bare bony feet with sand sticking all over them. Walking along a beach. In one of those old-fashioned swimming suits with bloomers and a sailor collar.

Her office was also the nurse's office when we had a nurse. It was all icky green tile floors and walls, with a cot in the corner for sick kids. The walls had posters about the four basic food groups and how to lift with your leg muscles, not your back. I didn't like the smell of the place, and I certainly didn't like being sent there for being off my nut.

There was nothing wrong with my head. It was Doug who needed help.

Dr. Feete wasn't into smiling like Mr. Ebersole. She pointed me into a chair, made a church steeple out of her fingers, and took her opening shot.

"I understand you're having a little trouble with reality, um, Dagmar." She had to look at her note pad to get my name.

"Yes, ma'am."

"Play it cool with this one," Doug advised. "Agree with whatever she says."

I looked around and caught a glimpse of him in the fish tank sitting on the bookcase behind her desk. I riveted my eyes on Sandy Feete's and held

61

them there, and blocked out her name so I wouldn't start giggling again.

"Tell me, um, Dagmar, how are things going for you at home?"

"At home?" I wasn't expecting that one. "At home. Well, let me think. Um, everything's okay at home. Except I have to share a room with GeorgeAnn, that's my little sister, and she drives me up a wall. But that doesn't have anything to do with . . ."

"You feel a sense of rivalry with your sibling? Is that it?"

"No, with my sister. GeorgeAnn. She's always hogging the limelight and getting into my stuff. And she listens in when I'm trying to . . ."

"How about your father? How do you feel about your father, Dagmar?" She seemed to be having a little trouble with my name, with keeping a straight face when she said it. Listen, she was in no position to laugh at other people's names. Not with a handle like Sandy Feete. If I'd been her I would have gotten married, first chance I had. You could always dump the husband if you didn't like him and go on using his last name.

"My father? He's fine. His back goes out if he's not careful, but mostly he's fine."

"But how do you *feel* about him?"

I looked at her, puzzled. "Fine. How am I supposed to feel?"

"You tell me," she said.

I didn't say anything. I couldn't think what she wanted me to say. I cleared my throat. "The reason I was talking to myself in the restroom . . ."

"How many siblings do you have, Dagmar?"

By now I had sibling figured out. "Oh. Sisters and brothers, you mean. Two sisters, three brothers."

"Six. That's a rather large family." She frowned. "And are you the oldest?"

"Yes," I said.

"Um hmm. Um hmm. And how do you feel toward, say, the youngest sibling?"

"That would be Delight, my baby sister. She's okay except if I have to change her diapers when they're stinky. And she's getting to where she pulls stuff over a lot, so we have to watch out for lamps and tablecloths and things like that."

"Yes, but how do you feel about her personally?"

I stared. I couldn't believe such a dumb question was coming out of a doctor. "Personally? She doesn't have any personally yet, she's only fourteen months old. I thought we were supposed to be talking about why I was talking to a fantasy boyfriend in the restroom."

"Don't push it," Doug bubbled at me. "Let her talk about what she wants to talk about. She's the doctor, you're only the nutcase."

"In other words," Dr. Feete said, "you would like to deny the existence of this sibling who is stealing the parental attention that you feel rightfully belongs to you, isn't that right? So you pretend your sister doesn't exist."

"No," I yelled, "my problem is pretending Doug *does* exist." For crying out loud, what was so hard about that? She wasn't getting with the program at all here.

To make my yelling louder, she lowered her voice to hardly a whisper and said, "I understand, Dagmar, believe me. I don't feel that there is anything seriously wrong with you at this time"—she stressed that, like my sanity could blow south with the next breeze—"but you must face reality."

Doug made fish lips at me. I tried to ignore him.

"Yes, ma'am. Face reality."

"You must understand that your baby sibling is a very real person, she does exist, and you will have to cope with that reality as you go through life. Try to understand that parents do have enough love to stretch over any number of siblings, but that it might not seem that they're sharing their time equally. That's usually because the younger ones need more care than older children."

"Yeah, she needs to have diapers changed forty times a day."

"That is reality, Dagmar."

"Yes ma'am."

"You may go back to class now, and any time you feel like talking this out with me, I'm always here for you. You know that, don't you? Any time you need me, for anything that's bothering you. As long as it's Monday afternoons, one to three P.M."

When I got off the bus at the post office, Daddy was just chugging up the street on his little orange town tractor with the mower blade on the side. Heading out to mow the weeds along the highway, he told me with hand signals. I nodded yes, I wanted to go along, and he slowed up for me to stand on the hitch bar behind his seat.

We chugged around past home and I ran in, dumped my books, and got a big plastic bag from the kitchen. Mom was in the bedroom changing the reality of Delight's stinky diaper.

I rode the hitch bar till we got out to the highway and Daddy let down the long mowing bar that stuck out to the side of the tractor and zapped off the weeds in a five-foot-wide swathe, along the edge of the paving.

Depending on where you live, you might have a different idea of highways from mine. Around New Berlin we've got two highways, County Road C and County Road CX. Where they cross each other is where they built the town. Neither one of them would be considered much of a highway if you live in New York or California or some place like that. They're just little two-lane roads with pink and purple crown vetch growing along the banks, and tan gravelly shoulders at the edge of the paving.

Occasionally a car or pickup truck goes by, and you always wave first, then look to see if it's someone you know. Generally it is.

I waded through the grass, down into the ditch, and started walking, looking for pop and beer cans. Our only rule was I had to stay behind Daddy's mowing bar so he didn't accidentally cut me off at the knees. I found an occasional can. Mondays were the best day for cans, especially after a nice weekend.

It felt good, walking along there with the sun warm but not hot, and with Daddy roaring slowly along ahead of me. He was company but without butting in.

"You missed one," Doug said, pointing to a can I hadn't seen, in a clump of cornflowers. He was riding on top of Daddy's mowing bar, floating on the dust cloud like some sheik stretched out on a sofa. He was up on one elbow, watching me.

"Thanks." I scooped up the can and dropped it into my sack. Five cents is five cents, and if I had a good day I might end up with enough to buy a new top at K-Mart before the party.

"Yes," Doug said. "What are we going to do about getting you a date for that party?"

"What?"

He shrugged. "Well, *I'm* not taking you, and you don't want to show up alone, do you? Listen, why don't you find somebody who fits my description and pass him off as me? Not that you're likely

66

to come up with this," he pointed to the dimple, "but you might dig up somebody who could pass."

"In your dreams. I have five days to come up with a sixteen-year-old hunk with black hair and blue eyes who'd go to a thirteen-year-old party with me? Get real. Where am I going to come up with somebody like that?"

"It pays to advertise," he said lightly. "Run a personal ad in the Cedar Rapids newspaper."

"Oh, yes. I have a clear vision of me advertising for a date."

"Desperate women do it all the time, sweet-heart."

"It costs money."

He pointed at my plastic bag with its growing load of five-cent-refund cans.

I stopped walking and looked helplessly at him. He shrugged, like he couldn't help the trouble I'd gotten myself into, then he started making fish lips again.

I sighed and plodded after him.

Nine

It was a very long weekend. It was also a very short week. I kept bouncing back and forth between being eager for the party and scared of the whole thing blowing up in my face.

I took Doug's advice about the newspaper ad, since he kept bugging me and bugging me about it. I sat around the cafe after school Tuesday until Mrs. Meyer quit noticing me, then I read the personal ads in the Cedar Rapids paper on the cafe counter. That gave me the general idea of what to say, and the price per word, which was a whole lot of pop cans' worth. But if I could get a passable Doug that way, it was probably worth it.

This was the ad I wrote: "WANTED, 16-YEAR OLD HUNK WITH DARK HAIR AND BLUE EYES, FOR

PARTY THIS SATURDAY NIGHT. MUST HAVE CAR. CALL DAGMAR, 555-3645."

I would have said more, but that was all I could afford. I ran my ad over to the post office with a money order I'd bought at the bank with my can money and got there just as the truck was picking up the last mail for the day. That should get it into Friday's paper, I figured.

For the rest of the week I just tightrope-walked from lie to lie. I told Shelly that Doug wanted to come to the party, but he had something that might interfere and he wouldn't know till the last minute.

I told my family that Shelly was having a date-party and I'd probably be going alone but there was a chance she might be fixing me up with a cousin of hers from down by Manchester.

Daddy frowned a lot at that and said he'd feel better about it if he took me over there himself and came and got me, but I carried on, pleading and whining, till he agreed not to humiliate me that way. "But we'll have to check out this cousin before we turn you loose with him. What's his last name? I didn't think Harbaughs had any relatives down around Manchester."

I got around that with a lot of vagueness and danced away from the subject as fast as I could.

They always tell you honesty is the best policy, and now I could see why. Living a lie just plumb wears a person *out*. Living more than one lie at a time, forget it. It's harder than geometry.

After I'd paid for the ad, I didn't have a penny left. No new top from K-Mart to wear at the party. Also, no money to buy Shelly a present. I had to give her a gift certificate from Kountry Kut and Kurl for a free styling and trim and promise to pay Aunt Dorothy back as soon as I could.

Other than those problems, I got through the week okay. Doug kept showing up at school and trying to distract me in class, but I didn't actually get into trouble from it. Apparently word had gotten out on the teacher-grapevine that I'd been in to see Dr. Feete because I was having problems at home. So the teachers were a shade gentler toward me than usual if I seemed to be staring at a window and talking to it when I should have been paying attention.

At least Doug had the sense to stay out of the restroom.

Friday after school I ducked Shelly and Matthew when we got off the bus and zipped across the street to the cafe. There were a bunch of guys in there from the phone company crew, drinking coffee and hoo-hawing around.

Mrs. Meyer asked if I wanted something and I said no, just waiting for Daddy. She went back to her stool behind the counter and picked up her counted cross stitch. She does counted cross-stitch mottoes and then frames them and tries to sell them. They're hanging all over the cafe.

I tried to ease up to the newspaper, but one of the phone guys picked it up and started looking through it. He had the classified ads, too, wouldn't you know it. He browsed through the boat section, mumbling about looking for a canoe.

Finally he folded the section and started to lay it down where I could grab it. But then he looked again and started grinning.

"You guys ever read these get-acquainted ads in here? They kill me. People so desperate they have to advertise in the paper. Here, listen to this one. 'Handsome professional man, early sixties, loves skiing, tennis, travel, and romantic evenings. Seeking trim, open-minded lady in her twenties or thirties, for companionship or more.'"

Around the table went general grunts of superiority over the poor guy who had to advertise. I stared out the window and acted like I wasn't there.

Doug whispered, "The guy's got to be a loser. Nobody but losers ever run those ads."

I jerked up straight and opened my mouth to yell at him, "What about me, Bozo? This was your idea, don't forget."

"Here's another one," the phone guy went on, still reading from the paper. "Listen to this one. 'Wanted, sixteen-year-old hunk . . .'"

"Run for it," Doug yelled, and I bolted out of the cafe and across the street. I was halfway home before the guy got to the part that said my name and phone number.

Bigmouth jerk, I fumed. Mrs. Meyer would never have read any of those ads. No one else in town did, that I knew of. But now, thanks to the phone company repairmen and their hoo-hawing, the whole town was going to hear about that stupid newspaper ad. Mrs. Meyer would catch the "Dagmar" part, and she'd recognize the New Berlin phone number.

"Doug, I could kill you. I would just wring your neck if you had one! I'm never going to live this down. I'm going to have to move away, change my name, start life over again in a strange city. Probably get caught in a prostitution ring like the girl in that movie Sunday night. You're supposed to be my dream boyfriend. How could you *do* this to me?"

He appeared beside me and put his arm around my shoulders and walked in step with me, like I'd seen couples walking. I'd always wanted to have somebody to walk close with like that, maybe with our hands tucked in each other's back jeans' pockets. I got a huge ache in my throat, wanting that so much and having only Doug.

Doug said, "You can't blame this on me, you know. I'm just a projection from your own mind."

I nodded morosely. All of a sudden I felt like

72

bawling, what with the newspaper ad fiasco back there in the cafe, and now Doug talking like he didn't even like me anymore. What if I couldn't even hold on to a fantasy boyfriend? That would be the pits at the bottom of the pits, if I couldn't even keep Doug interested in me.

By late afternoon on Saturday, our house was full. Of course I couldn't ruin my life quietly and in private, oh no. Whatever disasters were waiting for me, they'd happen in front of Aunt Dorothy and Uncle Dean and Neese. And Aunt Gretchen, of course. There was a softball game at the park that afternoon and the Happy Bodies had creamed the St. Olaf Swingers, which is another softball team of course, not a rock band or whatever else you might have thought they were from the name.

We had a pick-up kind of supper, bowls of tuna and macaroni salad sitting out on the dining room table with ripped-open bags of potato chips, jars of pickles you had to fish out with your fingers, and a chocolate sheet cake left over from the church bake sale, where Dean and Dorothy had just been.

Neese had been working at the bake sale, too. She's always doing things like that in hopes of meeting guys, but of course what guy is going to go to a church bake sale? It's no wonder she never gets anybody. Her bait ain't the best and she's trolling the wrong waters, as Daddy would say.

After supper Neese followed me upstairs to the

bathroom to coach me in the fine art of leg shaving. I'd tried it that afternoon and didn't get anything but raw skin. I didn't know you had to be wet and soaped first.

We got the job done finally. The legs weren't so bad once I got the knack of letting the razor sort of float along. But under the arms it really got tricky. I couldn't see where I was going with the blasted thing and darn near took off the end of my nose a time or two.

I did feel very womanly, though, as I got out of the tub and admired my new legs. They even seemed to have a little more shape to them than they had going into the bath. There were a few little red nicks around the kneecaps and ankle bones; otherwise it was a good shave job.

I got dressed in my best white dressy blouse and a full skirt with pink flowers all over it. It was still too early to head over toward Shelly's, so when Neese had finished playing around with my hair and painting on eye shadow, we went back downstairs.

GeorgeAnn was playing the piano and singing at the top of her lungs. Cootie and Uncle Dean were wrestling around on the living room floor trying to figure out armlock holds. Aunt Dorothy and Mom were trying to get Delight to walk back and forth between their stretched-out hands. David and Deaney were on the floor, too, trying to run their monster cars up people's legs and getting

74

swatted at a lot. Daddy and Aunt Gretchen had their faces up close to the television screen trying to hear the sportscast on the six o'clock news.

Over all that racket, you wouldn't think a knock on the door could be heard, but it was. I looked over the mob, thinking maybe this was going to be a last-minute miracle date from the newspaper ad.

But it was some old guy standing there outside the screen door. He was a big dude, maybe fifty or sixty but trying to look young, which always makes me sick. He had his shirt unbuttoned way down and three gold necklaces hanging down to his bare beerbelly. He had fat jowls that needed a shave and bloodshot eyes with hounddroops to them.

Neese went to the door and opened it.

"Does a Dagmar live here?" the man asked.

Ten

The room got amazingly quiet, except for GeorgeAnn still bellowing out, "Up above the world so high, like a diamond in the sky," at the top of her lungs.

But Daddy could outdo her. He threw back his head and yelled, "Thank you, GeorgeAnn, you've delighted us long enough!"

She paused, then rushed through the last line before she swung herself around on the piano stool.

Cootie looked up at me from under Uncle Dean's armpit. They were still doing wrestling holds on the floor. "Oh yeah, Dag. I forgot to tell you. Some old guy called while you were in the bathtub. This must be him. I told him where our house was. She was shaving her legs," he said to the strange man outside the screen.

Neese stepped across the bodies on the floor and held open the screen door. The man came in, but he had a funny look on his face, like he wasn't sure he'd get out of the asylum alive. Well, could you blame him?

He looked around the room, fastened his eyes on Aunt Dorothy, and said, "Are you Dagmar?"

He held up a folded newspaper, and with a sinking heart, as they say, I knew my jig was up.

Everybody in the room stared at me. Even Delight, who had collapsed on her bottom on the floor when Mom and Aunt Dorothy let go of her. Even GeorgeAnn was staring at me, although she went on twisting back and forth on the piano stool by swinging her arms and legs in opposite directions.

"I'm Dagmar," I said. To die, to die.

The man did a double take and stared at me.

"*You* are the Dagmar that advertised for a sixty-one year old party-man?"

"What!?" Mom gasped.

"What!" Daddy yelled.

Aunt Gretchen turned away from the television just as they were giving the major league scores, which is really something, for her.

The boys all got very still, down there on the floor, sensing fun approaching.

Neese said, "Who are you?"

77

"Darryl Fenmacher. I called about a personal ad. Only I wasn't expecting Lolita here."

"Who's Lolita?" Cootie asked.

"You're not sixteen," I accused him. "The ad said a sixteen-year-old hunk with dark hair and blue eyes and a car. You don't look like any of that stuff."

"Wait a cotton-picking minute here," Daddy said. "What is this, anyway. Dagmar, did you put an ad in the newspaper? For a . . ." Words failed him. He just motioned toward Darryl, who was trying to subtly button up a few shirt buttons.

Neese said, "I thought you were meeting your secret boyfriend at the party, Dag. What did you need to advertise for one for?"

Mom said in a low thundery voice, "*What* secret boyfriend? Dagmar?"

Cootie and the little kids rolled around to sitting position on the floor, so they could stare at me better.

GeorgeAnn said, "Dagmar's been sneaking around with some boy, and so has Neesie. They were out in parked cars on Chicken Ridge, kissing."

Aunt Dorothy's jaw dropped open. "Denise? Is that true?"

"Of course not," Neese started crying, just like it was her who was in trouble, not me. "That was just some stupid lie Dagmar told because her and Shelly were messing around with a couple of boys

78

Shelly knew, and they didn't want you to know about it because they were too young. Only GeorgeAnn snooped and found out. *And told.*"

GeorgeAnn innocently swung herself back and forth on the piano stool.

Darryl opened the newspaper and squinted at it, then held it out at the end of his arms. "Oh," he said. "Six*teen*-year-old hunk. I thought it said sixty-*one*-year-old hunk. I'm only fifty-four, but I figured that would be close enough. And my hair used to be darker than this, and my eyes are sort of bluish green, see?"

But nobody wanted to go up close and see.

There was a moment of silence while everybody soaked up what was happening. Slowly Darryl's shoulders sagged, and he said, "Heck, I drove all the way up here from Cedar Rapids for this. Got my hair styled and everything. Look, a thirty-dollar blow-dry styling job." He turned his head all the way around.

"You got took," Aunt Dorothy said dryly. "I could have done better than that, wouldn't have charged more than fifteen."

"Really?" he said. "Are you a hair stylist? That might be worth the drive up, if I could get it done for fifteen."

Neese went over to him and stared at the curls on the back of his neck. I could see her plotting how she'd do it if she could get her hands on him.

"Never mind this guy's hairdo," Daddy bellowed. "What I want to know is why was my little girl advertising for men in a newspaper. You're not even thirteen yet."

"I know that," I yelled back. "Everybody keeps telling me that. Doug keeps . . ."

Oops. Open mouth; insert foot.

"Who is Doug?" Daddy asked with death threats in his tone.

I opened my mouth, but nothing came out.

Neese helped me out. "Doug is the guy she's been sneaking around with, Uncle Early. He's sixteen, and he's got his own car, and he lives down by Strawberry Point somewhere. He's a friend of the guy Shelly's been sneaking around with. Sorry you had to hear it from me."

She was not.

Darryl said, "What are you, twelve years old and you're hanging out with some sixteen-year-old punk? Don't you know any better than that?"

As if all this wasn't enough, I caught sight of Doug in the reflection in the front door window. "Punk," he fumed. "Where does this over-the-hill swinger get off calling me a punk?"

I rolled my eyes toward heaven, but there was no help for me there, either.

"Okay, look," I said, and everybody got quiet. "This whole thing is just stupid. I never had a boyfriend, Neese never had a boyfriend."

"I did so," she interrupted. "I went out three times with Jason Kemp."

"Neese never had the boyfriend I made up for her," I went on patiently. "Neither did Shelly. It was all just a big lie. Well, it was a little lie to start with. Shelly was bragging about Matthew Garms being crazy about her, and I just got tired of it, and before I could stop myself I'd made up this totally fictitious boyfriend. Doug."

Aunt Dorothy said, "Shelly'd best watch herself. Those Garmses aren't a bunch I'd want a daughter of mine getting involved with. And that Matthew don't have two brains to rub together. How they ever pass him on from one grade to the next I'll never know."

Daddy looked at me with a softer expression and said, "You made up a pretend boyfriend, Daggie? Was that it?"

Him being nice to me made me want to bawl. I nodded my head and said, "I didn't mean for it to get out of hand, and I sure didn't mean for him to get so real." I yelled that last part at Doug in the window.

Darryl waved his newspaper and said, "What's that got to do with you putting this ad in the paper? Don't you know you could get in real trouble doing that? Most of the guys who answer these ads are creeps and losers. You were just lucky it was me that answered, not one of them."

Doug bent over double, laughing at that.

I went on explaining. "See, the whole trouble was, Shelly decided to have this date-party, and of

81

course she expected me to show up with Doug, who doesn't exist and who refused to go to a kid party anyway. It was his idea to put the ad in the paper. I was trying to come up with a guy I could pass off as Doug, just for this party. See?"

"No," they all said in unison.

"Who is this Doug?" Mom demanded.

"I told you, I just made him up."

"Then how could he tell you to put an ad in a paper?"

I threw my hands in the air.

Darryl said, "Listen, kid, I'll go to the party as your date. I'll pretend to be this Doug."

I looked at him sadly. Sagging beerbelly, balding gray hair, bloodshot hound eyes. I shook my head. "You'd never pass the physical. But thanks anyway."

He got a little snitty at that. "Look, sister, I drove all the way up here for this, when I could have stayed home and watched the Lakers game tonight."

Aunt Gretchen came to life at that. "You a Lakers fan?" She stood up, stretched her quarterback bulk, and patted herself on the stomach, on her Happy Bodies team shirt.

"Am I a Lakers fan?" Darryl said. "Does a camel spit? Is the Pope Catholic? Does a hog grunt? Does a . . ."

Aunt Gretchen stepped over the legs on the floor and went up to him. "You like those Lakers,

82

huh? Did you see their last game, when old
Johnson . . ."

In another minute they were hoo-hawing and
arm punching, and in another minute after that
they were headed out the door, going down to the
Cellar, which is the town's one bar, to watch the
Lakers game on the television down there.

I walked the three blocks to the party in lonely
splendor, still shaking inside from all the fuss and
furor. Thanks to Daddy being on my side, I'd gotten off pretty lightly, but still it had been a scene
I'd remember for a long time.

I walked along trying to keep my arms down so
my blouse would stay tucked in at the sides. It was
a cheap blouse without much tail to it. Nothing I
was wearing felt right, my legs had little stings all
over from the razor nicks, and even my hair felt
ugly. I was having to go from a first-class family
tear-up, right into my first date-party, without a
date or even any self-confidence.

I had a feeling shaved legs weren't going to be
enough to get me through the night.

Eleven

You know how, when you've looked forward to something really hard, it's always a disappointment? And you know how, when you've dreaded something for a long time it's always not as bad as you were dreading? Like having a dentist appointment for three weeks and then only needing cleaning and one small filling?

Well, this party turned out to be like the cleaning and one small filling. Not as terrible as I was afraid of, but also not wonderful. In fact it was a total bomb of a party, as far as I was concerned.

All it was was me and Shelly, Kim Hill and Tracey Crandall and Beth Beamer who couldn't get dates, Matthew Garms and Troy Jasper who is even a worse jerk than Matthew.

Shelly was all dressed up in this white slacks outfit with a black and white and turquoise top, and she had her hair kind of up in a twist at the back. She looked really great, except for the fake smile from trying to pretend it was a good party. I felt sorry for her.

And nobody wanted to do anything, that was the worst of it. I mean, the girls wanted to dance, but Matthew kept hanging around with Shelly's dad talking about deer season, and Troy got hold of a video game and wouldn't let up on it all evening, and then he went home at nine.

A couple of times Shelly got Matthew to dance with her, but he kept saying he wasn't a good dancer, and he was right, he was awful. So after a while she just let him wander back to her dad, and the two of them ended up in the den watching the Lakers game.

Shelly sank down beside me on the sofa, and we sat there staring at the refreshment table, where the cheese was getting dried edges and the punch was turning its ice cubes to water.

"So what happened to Doug?" she said. "He couldn't make it?"

"No, mainly because there isn't any such person. I just made him up because I was jealous of you having Matthew."

We looked morosely toward the den, where the ballgame was making the only happy noises in the house.

"You *made up* a boyfriend? You really are weird, Dagmar. Heck, I never even knew you wanted one all that much."

I shrugged. "It wasn't just the boyfriend. I wanted, I don't know, a secret life. You know?"

She slumped down farther, like she did know how awful it was not to have any kind of excitement or romance in your life.

Then she grinned. "Hah. You did have a secret life. All this week. The secret was, there *wasn't* any secret."

We had a good laugh over that, and that made me feel better.

I more than half expected Doug to show up in the punch bowl or somewhere, but he didn't. Possibly I was outgrowing him, I thought.

After the Lakers game Matthew came out of the den, and for a while we played jackpot Monopoly, and at eleven I got sleepy and started home.

Maybe where you live a young girl wouldn't walk home alone at eleven at night, but here in New Berlin nobody thinks anything about it. It was a dark, quiet, familiar walk that I'd been doing for years, Shelly's house to my house; one block down a hill, one block on the flat, past Main Street and across the bridge, then the last uphill block to my house.

I was coasting down the first block, slapping my feet on the sidewalk for the sound of it, when Doug showed up beside me.

"Huh. I thought I'd outgrown you. Didn't see you at the party anywhere."

"Oh, I was there, casing the joint. That was the dullest party I ever saw. A keg of beer would have livened it up."

"Some decent boys would have, too."

"Well, what can you expect, at your age?" he said in his superior voice.

"Look, Bozo, I've had about enough from you. You come into my fantasy, you start out being all sweetness and light, oh yes, don't interrupt me now, I'm on a roll."

I walked faster and talked faster. "You come waltzing into my life like God's gift, charm the socks off me, and then you start coming on with all this put-down stuff. I'm not smart enough for you, I'm not pretty enough for you, I'm too young. If I wanted that kind of treatment I could get it from a real guy."

As I walked up onto the bridge I could see old Charlie standing there staring down into the river. He wanders around town at all hours of the night; nobody thinks anything of it. He turned and looked at me. "Who you talking to, girl?"

"I'm talking to myself, Charlie," I yelled. "Don't interrupt a private conversation. I'm talking to myself. Why don't you try it some time?"

He turned away, muttering, "Kids never used to smart off to their elders when we was kids, did they? Nope, they sure didn't."

Off the bridge and in the last uphill block before home. Doug said, "Look, if you want to break it off, just say so. I can do better than you, you know. That Shelly is cute."

I sighed, exasperated. "Look. Doug. The whole point of having a fantasy boyfriend is so you can make him just the way you want him. Like faithful! Like adoring! Like, at the very least, thoughtful enough not to get you into trouble at school. You are *none of the above.* So just get out of my head! I don't ever want to see you or hear from you again."

And I didn't.

But you know what? You may not believe this, but Shelly and I were down by the river Sunday afternoon, and Matthew went past on his four-wheeler and Shelly never even looked at him.

"What's with you and Matthew?" I asked her.

She shrugged. "Oh, I don't know. I just lost interest in him, I guess. I had a dream last night, about this absolutely darling guy, and it was so real I couldn't believe I was dreaming. He had dark wavy hair and the bluest eyes, and these long curly eyelashes . . ."

"And a dimple like John Davidson's?"

She stared at me. "Yes, as a matter of fact. And this darling smile, and all through church this morning I kept imagining that he was talking to me, telling me how beautiful I looked with the sun shining through the stained glass windows on my hair."

I rolled my eyes toward heaven.

"I know he was just a dream," she went on, "but somehow, compared to him, old Matthew didn't look so hot anymore. Boy, if I could ever meet a guy like . . ."

Her head jerked to the side, and she stared down into the water, like she was seeing something in there.

I'll bet you a dollar somebody was making fish-lips at her.